Leapfrog Learners

Castles

by Annabelle Lynch

W

First published in 2012 by
Franklin Watts
338 Euston Road
London
NW1 3BH

Franklin Watts Australia
Level 17/207 Kent Street
Sydney
NSW 2000

Copyright © Franklin Watts 2012
Picture credits: istockphoto: front cover.
BAL, London/Superstock: 6;
Corbis/Superstock: 11 ;
BL/Heritage Images/Imagestate: 12;
Shutterstock: front cover inset, 8, 15, 16, 18;
Alamy: 5, 21.

A CIP catalogue record for this book is
available from the British Library.

Dewey number: 728.8'1

ISBN 978 1 4451 0325 9 (hbk)
ISBN 978 1 4451 0333 4 (pbk)

Series Editor: Melanie Palmer
Picture Researcher: Diana Morris
Series Advisor: Catherine Glavina
Series Designer: Peter Scoulding

Printed in China

Franklin Watts is a division of Hachette Children's Books,
an Hachette UK company. www.hachette.co.uk

Contents

The words in **bold** can be found in the glossary.

What is a castle?

Castles are buildings from long ago. They were built to protect people from **enemies**.

Castles were made from stone so they lasted a long time.

6

Who lived in a castle?

A lord and lady, **servants** and **knights** all lived in the castle.

There were also animals such as horses and dogs.

Inside the castle

Inside a castle, there was a great hall. This was where everyone ate big meals or **banquets**.

Great halls were also good for dancing in.

The moat

A **moat** often went around a castle. People had to use a **drawbridge** to get across.

Moats were filled with water. They helped keep out enemies!

Under attack!

Castles were hard to attack. They had high, stone walls and towers.

Knights could fire arrows from the towers.

Dungeons

Prisoners were put into the dungeon. This was a dark room hidden deep inside the castle.

Dungeons were often dark, damp and cold.

Castle fun

Living in a castle could be fun. There were lots of games to play. Knights held **jousts**.

Knights tried to knock each other off their horses with long poles called lances.

Haunted Castles

Some castles may
be haunted! People
tell stories of **ghosts**
walking around castles.

Would you spend the
night in this castle?

Visit a castle

There are lots of castles that you can visit. Why not go to see a castle for yourself?

Which castle is nearest to you?

Glossary

Banquet – very big meal for lots of people

Drawbridge – bridge that can be lifted up

Enemy – someone who fights against you

Ghost – invisible spirit of a dead person

Joust – game played by knights with lances

Knight – soldiers who served a lord or lady

Moat – deep water around a castle

Servant – person working for a lord or lady

Websites:

http://primaryhomeworkhelp.co.uk/Castles.html
http://www.castlexplorer.co.uk/
http://www.castlefacts.info/

Every effort has been made by the Publishers to ensure that the websites are suitable for children, and that they contain no inappropriate or offensive material. However, because of the nature of the Internet, it is impossible to guarantee that the contents of these sites will not be altered. We strongly advise that Internet access is supervised by a responsible adult.

Quiz

1. Who lived in a castle?

2. Where would you find the dungeon?

3. What happened in a great hall?

4. What use was a drawbridge?

5. What game did knights play?

6. Why were castles built?

The answers are on page 24

Answers

1. A lord, lady, servants and knights
2. Deep inside the castle
3. Big meals and sometimes dancing
4. To reach a castle across a moat
5. Jousts
6. To protect people from enemies

Index